Little Gold Star

A SPANISH AMERICAN CINDERELLA TALE

Retold by ROBERT D. SAN SOUCI

Illustrated by SERGIO MARTINEZ

HarperCollins*Publishers*

To my wonderful friends
Debra, Michael, and Nicholas Steele
—R.S.S.

To Carmen, my beloved wife
—S.M.

AUTHOR'S NOTE

This story, well known in New Mexico and the Southwest, is adapted from tales of Spanish origin, though it has roots in such tales as "Cinderella" and narratives collected by the Brothers Grimm and other folklorists.
In addition to working with previously translated versions of the tale from such books as *Literary Folklore of the Hispanic Southwest,* by Aurora Lucero-White Lea, and José Manuel Espinosa's *Spanish Folk-Tales from New Mexico*, published in 1937 as Volume XX of the memoirs of the American Folk-Lore Society, I used new translations of several old Spanish-language texts that were reprinted in the American Folk-Lore Society volume.

Little Gold Star

Text copyright © 2000 by Robert D. San Souci
Illustrations copyright © 2000 by Sergio Martinez

Printed in Singapore at Tien Wah Press.

All rights reserved.

www.harperchildrens.com

Library of Congress Cataloging-in-Publication Data
San Souci, Robert D.
Little gold star: a Spanish American Cinderella tale /
retold by Robert D. San Souci; illustrated by Sergio Martinez.
p. cm.
Summary: A Spanish American retelling of the familiar story of a kind girl
who is mistreated by her jealous stepmother and stepsisters. In this version,
the Virgin Mary replaces the traditional fairy godmother.
ISBN 0-688-14780-1 (trade)—ISBN 0-688-14781-X (library)
[1. Fairy tales.   2. Folklore—New Mexico.]   I. Martinez, Sergio, ill.
II. Title.   PZ8.S248 Li 2000   398.2'09789—dc21   99-50290

10 9 8 7 6 5 4 3 2 1
❖
First Editon

*I*n what is now New Mexico, there was once a sheepherder named Tomás whose wife had died. He had an only child, Teresa. She kept house while he tended his flocks high in the hills.

Then a widow and her two daughters moved nearby.
The woman visited often, and one day she said to Tomás,
"Surely you are as lonely as I. Marry me, and make us
both happy."

When Tomás refused, the widow began to weep. Not
knowing what to do, Tomás agreed to be married.

Teresa cared little for the haughty woman or her vain daughters, Inez and Isabel, but she said nothing.

As soon as Tomás's new wife moved into the house, she made life a misery for him and Teresa. She nagged her husband so much, he stayed in the hills longer and longer. And while he was away, Teresa had to do all the chores.

On one rare visit home, Tomás brought his wife and stepdaughters gifts of flowers and oranges. To Teresa he gave a lamb with soft white fleece.

As soon as her husband returned to his flocks, Teresa's stepmother killed the lamb. Handing the heartbroken girl the fleece, she ordered, "Go wash this in the river, so I can make myself a soft pillow."

Teresa had no choice but to obey. As she scrubbed, a fish snatched the wool and swam away. Teresa tried to grab back the fleece but failed. Fearing her stepmother's anger, she began to weep.

Just then, a woman dressed in blue came by and asked, "Why are you crying?"

When Teresa told her, the woman said, "Go up to that little shack on the mountainside. Tend the old man and the child there and sweep the floor, and I will bring the fleece back to you."

Teresa climbed the path to the hut. Inside, an old man with tangled hair and beard dozed while a baby cried in his cradle. Teresa gently rocked the infant and sang a lullaby until he went to sleep. Then she combed the old man's hair and beard. Finally she swept the place clean.

Teresa did, and instantly the sky was filled with birds. They wept until she filled ten bottles with their tears. The second time she touched her star, the birds shed feathers like soft rain, while Teresa stuffed twelve mattresses. When she touched the star a third time, the birds flew away and came back, carrying delicacies of every sort.

Teresa's stepmother and stepsisters gazed in wonder
when they returned. Realizing that Teresa had been
blessed, the woman sent Miguel a letter agreeing to the
marriage.

Tomás returned in time to see his daughter married.
And the joy of the bride and groom touched everyone.
Gradually, Teresa's stepmother grew less disagreeable
and began to treat her as a daughter. Isabel and Inez
grew kinder, and the donkey ears and horns became
smaller, then finally disappeared.

Miguel and Teresa lived lovingly all their days. And
the little gold star remained a sign of heaven's blessing
on them and their children.